Published by Scholastic Inc.
90 Old Sherman Turnpike, Danbury, Connecticut 06816.

For information regarding permission, write to:
Disney Licensed Publishing
114 Fifth Avenue, New York, New York 10011.

ISBN 0-7172-6802-0

Designed and produced by Bill SMITH STUDIO.

Printed in the U.S.A.
First printing, August 2003

DISNEP
♦ PRINCESS

A Promising Day

A Story About
Keeping Promises

by **S.R. Baecker**
illustrated by
S.I. International

SCHOLASTIC INC.

New York   Toronto   London   Auckland   Sydney
Mexico City   New Delhi   Hong Kong   Buenos Aires

"Nakoma," Pocahontas whispered, gently nudging her best friend. "Wake up, you promised to go fishing with me."

"Fishing—today," Nakoma mumbled. "I'm ready—" Her voice trailed off as she fell asleep again.

"Come on," Pocahontas urged. "It's going to be a beautiful day."

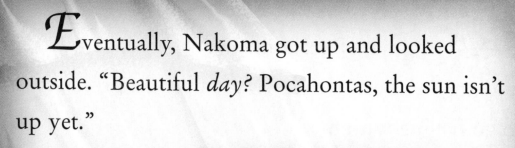

*E*ventually, Nakoma got up and looked outside. "Beautiful *day?* Pocahontas, the sun isn't up yet."

Then she sighed. "All right. A promise is a promise—let's go."

"Can we at least have breakfast?" Nakoma groaned.

"I brought it with me," assured Pocahontas, playfully pushing her friend outside.

"*I* love how quiet and peaceful the land is just before the sun rises," Pocahontas sighed. "All the animals that hunt at night are back in their nests and burrows. And the daytime hunters aren't awake yet."

"Me, either," Nakoma said, giggling.

Suddenly Nakoma grinned. "Come on—
race you to the river!" she yelled, as she darted
down the path.

While the girls were off fishing, Chief Powhatan was waking up with the sun. He began his daily morning walk through the village.

"Hmm, Pocahontas normally catches up with me by now," the chief thought. "She must be back home again."

"Oh, I wonder where she's off to now," the chief muttered quietly, peeking into their home. "I hope she remembers that she said she'd deliver food to the Weanocks today."

The chief walked back through the village.
But he didn't find Pocahontas. He walked to the
planting fields. But he didn't see her there.

Then he climbed the bluff overlooking the valley. Still, he didn't see her. "Pocahontas!" the chief's booming voice echoed through the valley.

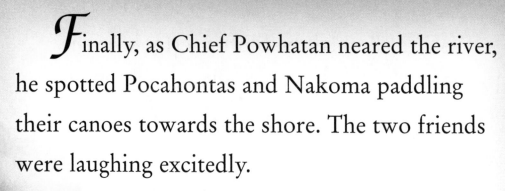

$\mathcal{F}$inally, as Chief Powhatan neared the river, he spotted Pocahontas and Nakoma paddling their canoes towards the shore. The two friends were laughing excitedly.

"Good morning, Father," Pocahontas said, hopping ashore. "What are you doing here?"

"*L*ooking for you," the chief said. "Did you forget your promise?"

"Of course not, Father," Pocahontas said.

"Look at how many fish we caught," Nakoma said, proudly displaying a string of fish.

"Hmm, it looks like you might have enough to feed the entire village for a week," the chief said, smiling.

"*I* thought I'd take the Weanocks some fish, too," Pocahontas said. "That's why we got up so early."

"Good," said the chief. "Remember, the food needs to be there before the sun falls below the trees." Then he walked back to the village.

"*I* told young Kleyo that I'd help him pick the corn this morning," said Nakoma as they reached the village. "See you later."

"Thanks for going with me," Pocahontas called out, hurrying home to pack the food for the Weanocks.

$\mathcal{P}$ocahontas and the chief packed quickly.

"Stop it, you two," Pocahontas said to Meeko
and Percy, gently nudging them off a bag of food.

"That should be plenty," the chief said, adding
some berries into the last bag. "That is," he said,
"if your friends don't eat too much along the way."

"Hello, Flit," Pocahontas said to her feathered friend. "I was wondering where you were." Then as Pocahontas neared the cornfield, she called, "See you later, Nakoma and Kleyo!"

"Wait!" shouted Kleyo.

"Where are you going, Pocahontas?" Kleyo asked, wishing he could go with her.

"Where the two wide rivers meet," explained Pocahontas, walking up to her friends. "I'm taking food to the Weanocks for their festival."

"Can I go with you?" Kleyo pleaded. "You told me you'd take me the next time. I can help, too. I'm the best paddler in the village!"

"Wait a minute, Kleyo," Nakoma said. "Didn't you promise to finish the field today?"

"Well, yes," he admitted. "But picking corn is just so boring."

"And didn't you tell your parents you'd get their permission before going anywhere on the river?" Nakoma added.

"Well, yes," Kleyo repeated. "But they'd let me go because I'm with Pocahontas. Let's just go. It'll be our secret! Please . . . *please!*"

Pocahontas knew Kleyo was right. She remembered that she had promised to take him the next time she went downriver. And the trip would be easier if he helped paddle because the canoe would be heavy with food.

But if she waited for Kleyo to finish the corn, would she be able to deliver the food on time?

*W*hat would a princess do?

Pocahontas thought for a moment and then exclaimed, "I have an idea!"

Pocahontas smiled at her young friend. "I'd like you to come, Kleyo. A great paddler like you would make the trip easier and faster. But I don't want you breaking your promises just to help me. It wouldn't be right."

"Nakoma, would you run back to the village and ask Kleyo's parents for permission?" asked Pocahontas, putting down her bag of food. "Then I could stay here and help Kleyo finish the field and still deliver the food on time," she added.

"All right," said Nakoma.

"Great idea, Pocahontas!" Kleyo shouted excitedly. "I bet we finish before Nakoma gets back!" he said, quickly picking corn again.

"Not if I take the shortcut and run like the wind!" Nakoma called out, as she ran off.

"Uh-oh, we'd better hurry and get this field done," said Pocahontas, laughing.

"There, that's the last ear of the last plant of the last row," Kleyo said. "We've finally finished!"

"*M*eeko, any sign of Nakoma yet?"
Pocahontas asked.

"Look, here she comes," Kleyo said, pointing
to the trail near the cornfield.

"Your parents said you can go as long as the field is finished and you're back before the sun sets," Nakoma said breathlessly. "Will you still make it in time, Pocahontas?"

"With Kleyo being the best paddler in the village, we will," said Pocahontas.

"*S*ee, I knew they'd let me go with you,"
Kleyo said. "We should've just gone."

$\mathcal{P}$ocahontas stopped at her canoe. "Kleyo, I think you're missing the point," she explained patiently. "Your parents trust you *because* you keep your promises. That's why they're letting you go."

Then Pocahontas and Kleyo climbed into the canoe. Kleyo quickly grabbed a paddle just as Nakoma pushed them off from shore.

"Now let's hurry so we can keep my promise to deliver this food," Pocahontas said, smiling.

The End